Oi! Get off our Train

John Burningham

RED FOX

Other books by John Burningham

Avocado Baby	Simp	*Little Books*
Aldo	Seasons	The Dog
Courtney	Time to get out of the Bath, Shirley	The School
ABC	Come Away from the Water, Shirley	The Friend
Albert	Would You Rather?	The Baby
Cloudland	The Shopping Basket	The Cupboard
Grandpa	Where's Julius?	The Snow
Trubloff	Humbert	The Rabbit
Humbert	Oi! Get off our Train	The Blanket
Harquin	Mr Gumpy's Outing	
Borka	Mr Gumpy's Motor Car	

For Chico Mendes who tried so hard to protect the rainforest of Brazil

A Red Fox Book

Published by Random House Children's Books
20 Vauxhall Bridge Road, London SW1V 2SA

A division of Random House UK Ltd
London Melbourne Sydney Auckland
Johannesburg and agencies throughout the world

Copyright © 1989 John Burningham

1 3 5 7 9 10 8 6 4 2

First published in Great Britain by
Jonathan Cape Ltd 1989
Red Fox edition 1999

Printed in Singapore

RANDOM HOUSE UK Limited Reg. No. 954009

ISBN 0 09 985340 X

Oi! Get Off Our Train

"You aren't still playing with that train are you?
Get into bed immediately. You know you have to be up
early for school tomorrow."

"Here is your pyjama-case dog. I found it under a cushion in the sitting room. Now, settle down and go to sleep."

"We're ready to go now.
Don't make too much noise with the shovel."

"If there's time we can have a picnic."

"It looks as if it is going to be foggy ahead.
If it is we can play ghosts."

"Oi! Get off our train."

"Please let me come with you on your train.
Someone is coming to cut off my tusks,
and soon there will be none of us left."

"It's going to be a very hot day.
If it is we must find somewhere for a swim."

"Oi! Get off our train."

"Please let me come with you on your train.
If I stay in the sea I won't have enough to eat
because people are making the water very dirty
and they are catching too many fish,
and soon there will be none of us left."

"I think there is going to be a strong wind.
If there is we can all fly kites."

"Oi! Get off our train."

"Please let me come with you on your train.
I live in the marshes and they are draining
the water out of them. I can't live on dry land,
and soon there will be none of us left."

"It looks as if it is going to rain soon.
If it does we can all muck about with umbrellas."

"Oi! Get off our train."

"Please let me come with you on your train.
They are cutting down the forests where I live,
and soon there will be none of us left."

"I think there's enough snow now.
If there is we can all throw snowballs."

"Oi! Get off our train."

"Please let me ride on your train. I live in the Frozen North
and somebody wants my fur to make a coat out of,
and soon there will be none of us left."

"If it does not stop snowing soon
we are going to get stuck."

"We must go back now.
I have to get to school in the morning."

"You must get up immediately
or you will be late for school.

There are lots of animals in the house.
There's an elephant in the hall,
a seal in the bath,
a crane in the washing,
a tiger on the stairs
and a polar bear by the fridge.
Is it anything to do with you?"